D0016498

LITTLE LOCOMOTIVE

English translation by Virginia Allen Jensen

Weekly Reader Children's Book Club presents

LITTLE LOCOMOTIVE

by Ib Spang Olsen

Coward, McCann & Geoghegan, Inc.

New York

First American Edition 1976
Illustrations copyright © 1963 by Ib Spang Olsen
English translation copyright © 1976 by International Children's Book Service ApS

All rights reserved. This book, or parts thereof, may not be reproduced in any form without permission in writing from the publishers. Published simultaneously in Canada by Longman Canada Limited.

SBN: GB-698-30616-3   SBN: TR-698-20364-x

Library of Congress Catalog Card Number: 75-13191

Weekly Reader Children's Book Club Edition

"I never get anywhere."
The little locomotive sighed.
"Day in and day out,
back and forth
on the same old tracks.
Push one car this way,
pull two cars that way.
I wish I could take
a long, long trip."
Just then the engineer came.
He filled the boiler with water
and he fired it with coal.
Soon smoke and steam puffed
out of the stack.
"Now I'll clean the windows
and we can get started," he said.

He went to fetch some rags.
"Duuuut!" said the engine and drove off by itself.

TOOOOOT!

The engineer ran as fast
as you can ride a bicycle,
but he couldn't catch up with it.

"*Dadagum, dadagum,*" sang the engine
and sped away down the rails.
It headed for the station.
It was going somewhere!

Many people
were waiting
for the train.
People with baggage
and people
without baggage.
Children, grown-ups,
a dog, and two dolls.
"Here comes
the local train,"
a little girl shouted.

The people picked
up their bags,
but it wasn't the
local train at all.
It was the locomotive,
and it didn't stop.
It rushed
through the station,
out of the city,
and into the country.

"*Dadagum, dadagum, dadagum.*
This is fun. This is fun. This is fun."
The little engine looked around

and saw on the right
some doves in flight,

a man with a sack,
and a chimney stack,

an empty pail,
a mallard's tail,

a fine little town,
and clouds around,

a boy against
an electric fence,

a cabin and
a heap of sand.

It saw a calf,
but only half,

a brown-eyed cow
with a wrinkled brow.

It saw a colt
buck and bolt.

It saw a smith.
It saw a goat.

It saw a sheep
with a heavy coat,

some hens and geese,
a loaded truck,

a berry bush,
a dog amuck,

a girl named Jean,
painting green,
a man called Fred,
and a fox that fled.

"Oh happy day,
I'm on my way,"
sang the little engine.

"Dadagum, dadagum, dadagum."

The engine sang all the way to the next station.
The stationmaster was switching the track. *Clunk!*

He moved the little engine on to a sidetrack.

The engine shot right off
the end of the sidetrack.
Clatter, rumble, bump.
It plowed into the ground
and was about to tip over—
but it didn't.

It crossed a field.
It crossed a ditch
and rolled right up
Mrs. Jensen's
front walk.

MRS. A
JENSON

It couldn't stop
and it couldn't steer.
It had to go through the kitchen door. *Boom!*

Mrs. Jensen didn't turn around
to see who it was.
She was busy
baking a cake,
so she just said,
"Dry your feet on the mat!"
It was muddy outside.

The engine backed up. *Screech!*
It dried its wheels on the mat.

Round and round they went
and tore the mat to shreds.

That made Mrs. Jensen turn around.
"Oh, no!" she screamed.
And *that* scared the engine.
It chugged right
out the other door
without saying good-bye.

Choo! It ran into the clothesline
and picked up Mrs. Jensen's laundry—
poles, line, clothes, and all.

Swoop!
It picked up
a pine tree, too.

Splash! It ran through a pond,
and everything got wet.
Nearby, two men were
working in a field.
"What do you think of that?"
one of them said.
"Mrs. Jensen's laundry
is out for a ride."
"Yes, and so is a Christmas
tree," the other said.
"That's odd," they agreed.

The little locomotive
came to a road
leading to a big town.
Now it was
getting somewhere.

The people
in the town
were surprised
to see an engine

on their main street,
wearing
laundry and a
Christmas tree.

It puffed its way
right out of the town.
The road turned,
but the engine couldn't.

Bump-a-dump, bump-a-dump, it rumbled

across a field
and onto
a new track.
It was speeding right along.

"*Dadagum, dadagum, dadagum,*" the engine hummed.
Suddenly it got dark. *This is no fun,*
thought the engine. *I can't see anything.*

But the tunnel was short,
and the next moment
it could see again.
It was high up in the air
and far, far below
was the water.
It crossed the bridge
and came to a little house.
"I think I've been here before.
I know that house," it said
and hopped
and skipped
and jumped.

And the laundry flew off—poles, line, clothes, and all.
The clothes were all dry,
ready for Mrs. Jensen to put away.

The tree fell off by the electric fence.
The boy was glad. He could save it for Christmas.

I must be nearly home, the engine thought.
It was running out of steam.
There was no one to stoke the boiler.

The engine chugged slower and slower.
Chug . . . chug . . . chug . . .chug.

With the last chug
it stopped, exactly where it had started.
The engineer was still there, looking surprised.

The little locomotive was *home* again.

The railroad company fixed Mrs. Jensen's doors and gave her a new doormat to keep her happy.

Now the little locomotive spends its days—and even nights—chugging back and forth in the railroad yards. And whenever it rains, it thinks about the time it dried its wheels on Mrs. Jensen's doormat.